BRENDA THE DO-IT-YOURSELF BROWNIE

Born in Middlesex, Mick Gowar is an author, poet, songwriter and performer. After finishing college, he worked in journalism and public relations, where he helped promote a computerized doorbell that played ten different tunes. He has been a full-time writer since 1986, and lives in Cambridge.

Also by Mick Gowar

BILLY AND THE GHASTLY GHOST
BILLY AND THE MAN-EATING PLANT

Mick Gowar

BRENDA
THE
DO-IT-YOURSELF
BROWNIE

Young Piper Original

PAN MACMILLAN
CHILDREN'S BOOKS

First published 1992 by Pan Books Ltd,
Cavaye Place, London SW10 9PG

1 3 5 7 9 8 6 4 2

© Mick Gowar 1992

The right of Mick Gowar to be identified as author of this
work has been asserted by him in accordance with the
Copyright, Designs and Patents Act 1988.

ISBN 0 330 32212 5

Phototypeset by Intype, London
Printed in England by Clays Ltd, St Ives plc

ONE

'It's not fair! It's not fair!' yelled Brenda at the top of her voice. She stamped her foot in fury. 'You told me that as soon as I was seven I could join the Brownies – you *promised*!'

'I know I did, dear.' Her mum sighed. 'But I've just phoned Brown Owl, and she says she's terribly sorry but the Brownie Pack is full up. They can't take another single Brownie until the autumn.'

It was the day after Brenda's seventh birthday. She'd been looking forward to it for months, because seven was the age to start Brownies. But instead of being one of the best days of her life – as she'd imagined – it had turned out to be one of the worst.

For as long as she could remember, Brenda had wanted to be a Brownie. For the past year, she'd watched enviously from the window as the bigger girls had hurried up the road on Monday nights in their smart uniforms, heading for the church hall. She'd sometimes seen them, on warm summer evenings, playing complicated running-and-hiding games on the village green. And at the Christmas Fayre she'd spent ages watching the Brownies selling home-made jams, old books and broken toys from two wooden tables decorated with tinsel and plastic holly – just like proper shop-ladies, with real money! And she'd thought to herself: 'As soon as I'm seven, I'll be able to do that!'

Brenda was sure that being a Brownie was the most exciting thing in the whole world. But now – on the very day she was old enough to be a Brownie – everything had gone wrong.

'I'm sorry, love,' said Mum, 'but there's nothing anybody can do – the Pack is full up.'

'But couldn't they take just *one* more,' pleaded Brenda desperately. 'I wouldn't take up much room. I'd be so quiet, they wouldn't even know I was there! Oh please, Mum. Phone Brown Owl and ask her again – *please*.'

But Mum shook her head, sadly. 'It wouldn't do any good, Brenda,' she said. 'Brown Owl hasn't got enough helpers to take on any more Brownies – even very small ones. She isn't allowed to. But she did say you could start in the autumn – for certain. That's only a few months – it's not long to wait—'

But Brenda was too upset to listen to any more excuses. She stomped out of the living room and up the stairs, trying as hard as she could not to cry.

'Brownies are brave,' she repeated to herself, as she got to her bedroom. 'Brownies don't cry.' But then she remembered that she wasn't a Brownie, and she wouldn't be a Brownie for months and months and months!

Brenda ran across her room, threw herself dramatically on to her bed, and began to howl.

A minute or two later the bedroom door opened and Mum came in. She walked over to the bed and sat down next to the sobbing Brenda. She put her arms round Brenda, but Brenda made herself as stiff and lumpy and uncuddly as she could.

'Come on, love, cheer up,' Mum murmured in a soothing voice. She stroked Brenda's hair and made soft cooing noises.

Gradually, Brenda relaxed. After a

few minutes, she found – to her surprise – that her tears had stopped. She went on making sobbing noises, but she soon got tired of that, too. Finally, she sat up on the bed.

Mum gave her a hanky. Brenda wiped her eyes and blew her nose loudly.

'Feeling a bit better now?' asked Mum.

Brenda gave a last, satisfying sniff and nodded.

'I know how disappointed you are,' said Mum, 'but you will be a Brownie in the autumn – Brown Owl promised. It's only a few months, and in the meantime you can still read all your Brownie books and draw all your lovely pictures of Brownies . . .'

Mum pointed to the wall beside Brenda's bed. On it were six drawings of Brownies, stuck to the wallpaper with Blu-Tack. Brenda

had spent hours copying them from Brownie books which she'd borrowed from the library. Brenda had only finished the last one that morning. It was a picture of a girl's face. The girl was wearing a brown bobble hat. She had very round, bright blue eyes, and her mouth was wide open to show two rows of gleaming white teeth. Underneath the face Brenda had written: 'BRONES ARE WIDE AWEAK.'

'I've got a good idea,' said Mum brightly. 'Why don't we read another chapter of your new Brownie book tonight, after your bath?'

She picked up the copy of *The Brownie Guide Handbook* from the floor by Brenda's bed. (It had been Brenda's birthday present from her little brother, Sean.)

Mum flicked through it until she got to a page which seemed to interest her.

'I've just had another idea,' said Mum. 'You can always *practise* being a Brownie. Just because you aren't a member of a Brownie pack yet, it doesn't mean you can't do some of the things that Brownies do.'

Brenda looked very confused.

Mum handed Brenda the *Handbook*. 'Can you read what it says on that page?' Mum pointed.

'*Brownies help at home*,' Brenda read aloud.

'Good,' said Mum, smiling. 'So, why don't you start now?'

'How do you mean?' asked Brenda, still puzzled.

'You can come downstairs and help me lay the table for tea,' Mum replied with a grin.

Later that evening, after Brenda's bath, Mum read her a chapter from *The Brownie Guide Handbook*.

It was called 'The Brownie Story'. It was about two children – a girl of about Brenda's age and her little brother, who was about the same age as Brenda's little brother Sean – who tried to find a real Brownie, a sort of helpful pixie, to help their mum with the housework. The two children went to the wood and asked the Wise Owl where they could find a Brownie. The Owl told them to go to the pool in the wood, turn round three times and say:

'Twist me and turn me and show me the elf.
I looked in the water and there saw . . .'

And when they looked in the water, they would see a Brownie whose name would fill in the missing word of the rhyme.

The children did what the owl told them, but when they looked into the

water all they saw were their own
reflections. They'd been very
disappointed, until the Wise Owl
told them that *they* could be the
Brownies. The missing word of the
rhyme, the Owl explained, was
'. . . myself!'

So the two children had gone
home, got up very early next
morning, and done all the housework
for Mum – just like a proper
Brownie would have done.

'Were those children *really* the first
Brownies?' asked Brenda, as soon
as Mum had finished reading. 'Is
that how the Brownies really
started?'

'Well, not exactly . . .' Mum
glanced through the picture story
again. 'It's more like a fairy story.
There aren't really talking owls, are
there? . . . And children don't really
get up at dawn to do all the
housework,' she added with a wistful

sigh, 'though it would be nice if it were true.'

'Yes, but if it isn't true – then it must be a fib,' said Brenda. 'And Brownies mustn't tell fibs – ever!' Brenda was shocked at the thought of a fib in *The Brownie Guide Handbook*.

'I don't think it's a fib, exactly . . .' Mum looked perplexed. 'It's rather difficult to explain. I don't think the story is meant to be . . . well, the true story of how the Brownies actually started. I think it's meant to show you how *you* can be a good Brownie – by thinking of others and helping people. Do you understand?'

'Hmmm . . .' Brenda still looked doubtful. She looked at the pictures again.

'But one of the Brownies in the story is a boy,' she said, pointing at the last picture. 'There aren't any boy Brownies, are there?'

'No,' agreed Mum. 'But I think the story is trying to say that *anyone* can help their mum with the housework. What the story is really saying is that you don't have to belong to a Brownie Pack at all to behave like a good Brownie – you don't even have to be a girl; boys can be just as kind and helpful as Brownies. Is that a bit clearer?'

'I think so,' said Brenda. 'But—'

'That's enough questions for tonight,' said Mum wearily. 'It's time to go to sleep. Good night, love. Happy dreams,' and she kissed Brenda.

'Good night, Mum.'

Mum went downstairs. But Brenda lay awake, thinking about the story and all the things Mum had said.

'They didn't have uniforms, or belong to a proper Brownie Pack,'

Brenda muttered to herself. 'But they *were* Brownies – Mum said so.'

She ran through the story once again, in her head: 'A big sister, and a little brother . . .'

By the time Brenda fell asleep, she felt much happier. It didn't matter so much any more that Brenda couldn't join the Brownie Pack until the autumn; the story, and Mum's explanations, had given Brenda an idea – a very good idea!

TWO

Two days later, on Saturday morning, Brenda put her idea into action. The idea was really quite simple, as all good ideas are: she and Sean would form their own Brownie Pack, just like the children in the story. But better. They were going to be a *proper* Brownie Pack, with uniforms, the Brownie Promise – the lot! Brenda had worked it all out in her mind.

As soon as breakfast was over, Brenda's Brownies began their first Pack Meeting in the garden. They were dressed in the nearest things to Brownie uniforms that Brenda could find. Brenda was wearing her brown corduroy trousers and brown-and-yellow striped T-shirt, and she had an old brown bobble hat on her head.

Sean was wearing his Spiderman pyjamas and his gun-belt. Brenda was holding her copy of *The Brownie Guide Handbook* and trying to make Sean behave like a Brownie. It wasn't easy.

'I'll explain again,' said Brenda, as patiently as she could. 'I'm the Sixer, so that means you have to do what I tell you – got it?'

'Does that mean we can't play War?' asked Sean.

'No,' said Brenda.

'Or Cowboys and Indians?'

'No,' said Brenda.

'Or Cops and Robbers?'

'No,' said Brenda.

'So what *are* we going to do?' asked Sean. He couldn't think of anything that was left.

Brenda consulted her book again. 'We're going to promise to do our duty to God, to serve the Queen, and to help other people.'

'What sort of helping?' asked Sean, suspiciously.

'Oh, things like dusting, doing the washing-up – that sort of thing.'

Sean had a better idea: 'Why don't we help people by shooting lots of baddies, and tying them up, and throwing them in jail?'

He pulled his cowboy gun out of its plastic holster and made 'Pyang! Pyang!' noises.

'*No!*' yelled Brenda, beginning to lose her temper.

'Then I'm not playing!'

Brenda was about to tell Sean what he could do with his stupid cowboy gun, but she just stopped herself in time. Without Sean there wouldn't be a Brownie Pack. She decided to try the sneaky approach.

'I'll give you some of my chocolate buttons if you'll play . . .'

'What chocolate buttons?' Sean was suddenly interested again.

'I bought some with my pocket money yesterday,' Brenda explained. 'They're upstairs in my bedroom.'

'And you'll give me some if I play Brownies?'

'Yes,' said Brenda.

'Honestly?'

'Cross-my-heart-and-hope-to-die,' Brenda promised.

'How many?' Sean had been tricked by Brenda before. Once he'd played Mummies and Babies, for a whole afternoon, for just one orange fruit gum.

'Lots!' replied Brenda. Sean had only learned to count up to five. After that, everything was 'Lots'.

'Give them to me first, then I'll play,' said Sean, cautiously.

'Half now, and half when we've finished,' suggested Brenda.

Sean thought about the offer for a moment.

'OK,' he agreed. 'But when we've finished playing Brownies, you've got to promise to play what I want – all right?'

'Promise!' said Brenda. She had the fingers of both hands crossed behind her back.

As Brenda was coming downstairs from her bedroom (with as few chocolate buttons as she thought she could get away with) she met Mum going up. Mum was carrying the vacuum cleaner.

'Will you and Sean be all right on your own for a while?' Mum asked. 'Only, I would really like to get the bedrooms cleaned before Dad comes back from the shops. I'll be upstairs if you do need anything, but I'd be *so* grateful if you could keep yourselves amused for an hour or so – without fighting!'

'We're playing Brownies in the garden,' Brenda explained.

'That's nice, dear,' said Mum. 'That sounds like a very good game.'

She carried on lugging the heavy hoover up the steep stairs. She stopped at the top, and turned back to Brenda.

'Remember, I'll be up here if you need anything – but try not to.'

'Don't worry, Mum,' said Brenda soothingly. 'You have to be good when you're being a Brownie.'

As Brenda reached the bottom of the stairs, the doorbell rang. She opened the front door. On the step stood Sylvia, her friend from next door. Sylvia was dressed in a frilly summer frock with puffed sleeves and a Peter Pan collar. In one hand she was holding a pink plastic pony with a long orange mane and a unicorn-style pimple on its forehead. In her other hand was a turquoise plastic comb.

'Hallo,' said Sylvia. 'Would you

like to play with me and Silverhooves?' She waved the garish creature under Brenda's nose. 'Isn't he *sweeeet?*'

'Er . . . yes,' agreed Brenda, doubtfully. 'But I can't – I'm playing with Sean . . .'

Then Brenda had another good idea.

'But you can play, too,' she added, quickly. 'We're making a Brownie Pack, would you like to join?'

'What's a Brownie Pack?' asked Sylvia. 'It's not like a mud pack, is it?'

'I don't think so . . .' said Brenda, uncertainly. 'What's a mud pack?'

'It's what my mum puts on her face,' explained Sylvia. 'It starts out all slimy and yucky and disgusting, and then it goes all dry and yucky and disgusting. It's to make her more beautiful.'

'Does it work?' asked Brenda.

'No,' said Sylvia, shaking her head.

'Well, a Brownie Pack's nothing like that,' said Brenda. 'It's like a kind of club, and you do good deeds and think of others. It's brilliant fun! Come on, I'll show you.'

Sylvia followed Brenda through the house and out into the garden.

'What do we do now?' asked Sylvia.

'Well, first we have to swear,' said Brenda.

Sylvia looked shocked. 'My mum doesn't let me use rude words,' she said.

'No, no – it's not that kind of swearing,' Brenda explained quickly. 'It's like a promise: you promise to be good, and help people . . . things like that. You see,' Brenda continued, in a confidential whisper, 'being in the Brownies is like being in a secret club – so you have to make a special promise.'

'Do you mean, like they do on TV: *I promise to tell the truth, the whole truth . . .* ?' asked Sylvia. 'Like on *Cagney and Lacey?*'

'Yes,' said Brenda, 'that sort of thing. You have to repeat after me . . . ' She looked at her *Brownie Handbook. 'I promise to—'*

'What about my chocolate buttons?' Sean interrupted. 'I'm not promising anything until I get my chocolate buttons!'

'Here you are,' said Brenda, reluctantly handing them over.

Sean crammed them all into his mouth at once.

'Are you ready?' asked Brenda.

Sylvia and Sean nodded.

'Right. *I promise to—'*

'Shouldn't we have a Bible, or something?' Sylvia interrupted.

'Why?' asked Brenda crossly. At

this rate, by the time Brenda's Brownie Pack started all the Brownies would be old enough to join the Guides – or, in Sean's case, the SAS.

'They do on *Cagney and Lacey*,' replied Sylvia, with a superior sniff. 'When someone's on trial or something, they always have to swear to tell the truth on the Bible – *everybody* knows that!'

Brenda consulted *The Brownie Guide Handbook* again. It didn't say anything about Bibles, but it did say that some Brownie Packs made their Brownie Promise around a Magic Pool.

'Just like the story about the First Brownies,' thought Brenda. 'And we are like those First Brownies, aren't we?'

Brenda *so* wanted to do everything properly. They obviously needed a pool to make their Brownie

Promises, the book said so. And it didn't have to be a large pool, either, because there were only three of them. There was just one snag: there wasn't a pool in Brenda's garden.

'Oh, well,' thought Brenda, 'we'll just have to make one!'

THREE

Sylvia refused point blank to have anything to do with digging a pool.

'This is my best dress!' she protested, smoothing out an imaginary wrinkle from the skirt. 'My mum only let me wear it today because I promised not to get it dirty. She'd be *furious* if I got all muddy.'

Brenda tried arguing with her, but Sylvia refused to budge. Eventually, Brenda fetched her's and Sean's seaside spades from the shed. They dug the pool, while Sylvia settled herself under the apple tree and began to groom Silverhooves with the turquoise plastic comb.

The digging was hard work, and it took a long time. Sean got bored after ten minutes, and Brenda had to bribe him with another handful of

chocolate buttons. Every so often, Brenda thought she noticed Sylvia looking at her with a sly grin on her face, but she decided to ignore it.

The digging took about an hour. Then Brenda and Sean filled the pool with water from the rain barrel beside the garden shed, taking it in turns with the small bucket from Sean's sandpit.

Once all the dirty work was over, Sylvia went to inspect the finished pool.

The pool was circular, and about a metre and a half across. It was right in the middle of the lawn.

'It doesn't look much like a Magic Pool to me,' said Sylvia, sniffily. 'It looks more like a muddy hole!'

Even Brenda had to admit she was right. For some reason that Brenda didn't understand, the water hadn't stayed in the pool as it was supposed to. Instead, it had soaked away into the soil, leaving nothing but a squelchy patch of mud at the bottom of the hole.

But Brenda wasn't going to be put off – not after all the hard digging she'd done.

'Well, I'm the Sixer and I say it's all right,' she said, defiantly. 'So, form a circle—'

Suddenly, Sean yelled, 'Can Tigger be a Brownie, too?' And without waiting for a reply, he rushed excitedly across the garden.

Tigger, their cat, had just crept through the gap in the fence from next door's garden. He'd been having a mid-morning snooze on the concrete patio that Sylvia's father had almost finished building. His route home had involved walking across something wet and sticky, and he didn't like it one bit.

Tigger was sitting by the fence, shaking his paws. He was trying to remove a thin coating of cement which was smeared over his pads and between his claws.

Before Brenda could say 'No', or Tigger could get away, Sean had grabbed the unfortunate cat and dragged him into the circle.

'Repeat after me – ' Brenda said quickly, before there were any more interruptions, '*I promise*—'

'I promise—' chorused Sean and Sylvia.

'*To do my best*—'
'To do my best—'
'*To do my duty to God*—'
'To do my duty to God—'
'*To serve the Queen*—'
'To serve the Queen—'
'*And help other people*—'
'And help other people—'
'*And to keep the Brownie Guide Law.*'
'And to keep the Brownie Guide Law.'

Brenda paused. '*And to always do what my Sixer tells me to*,' she added quickly.

It wasn't really part of the Brownie Promise, but Brenda had decided to put it in anyway. It seemed a wise precaution – especially after all the arguments and difficulties they'd had during the morning (not to mention most of a bag of chocolate buttons wasted on bribing Sean).

'And to always do what my Sixer tells me to,' intoned the other two Brownies solemnly.

'Now, do the Brownie salute,' said Brenda. 'Like this.' She showed them. Sylvia returned the salute smartly.

'I can't do it,' complained Sean. 'It's too difficult!' His salute looked like someone banging half a pound of sausages against the side of his head.

Brenda held down his thumb and little finger.

'Ow! That hurts!' Sean complained again. He finally managed a ragged salute.

'Does that mean we're Brownies now?' asked Sylvia.

Brenda consulted *The Brownie Guide Handbook* again. On the page after the Brownie Promise there was a picture of a Brownie Pack standing in a ring round their pool. One of the Brownies had just made her promise, and she was standing at the edge of the pool with her knees bent. As far as Brenda could see, the picture was perfectly clear: the new Brownie was just about to leap over the pool.

'Not quite . . .' said Brenda. 'First, you have to jump over the Magic Pool. Then you're a real Brownie. I'll go first, because I'm the Sixer.'

Brenda took one step back from the pool, and jumped across. The far side of the pool was a bit slippery, but she managed to jump without any difficulty.

'Now me!' yelled Sean eagerly, hoisting up his gun-belt.

'No,' said Brenda. 'Sylvia's next, because she's the Second.'

'Do I have to?' asked Sylvia.

'Yes,' said Brenda, firmly.

'Now?' asked Sylvia, with a worried frown. The pool suddenly looked a lot bigger than before.

'Yes,' repeated Brenda.

Sylvia took a deep breath. Then she took a step back. Then another step. She tried to measure the distance across the pool with her eyes. She took another two steps back, then another two.

'I can't do it,' she wailed.

'Of course you can,' called Brenda

from the far side of the pool. 'It's easy!'

Sylvia took two final steps back. Then she took another deep breath, and began her gigantic run-up.

But as she got closer and closer, the pool seemed to get bigger and bigger. Then, just when she was no more than half a metre from the edge, Sylvia lost her nerve completely. She tried to stop, but her feet kept sliding. She waved her arms frantically to regain her balance, but her feet just kept going. For an agonizing second, she teetered on the brink like a ballet dancer on points. Then, with a shriek and a loud *splat!*, Sylvia landed face down in the muddy puddle at the bottom of the pool.

'Owwwwwww!' she howled. 'I'm all wet . . . and look! My dress – it's *ruined*! My mum will kill me! Owwwww! Oooooooh!'

Sylvia's screams brought Mum rushing to the bedroom window.

'What's the matter?' she called down to the children. 'Are you all right, Sylvia?'

Then she saw the Magic Pool in the middle of the lawn.

'OH, NO!' she yelled. 'What *have* you done! Our beautiful lawn – ruined! You wait till your father gets home . . . !'

Brenda and Sean spent most of the rest of the day in their bedrooms, being very good and quiet.

Dad had been livid. And he'd put most of the blame on Brenda.

'I'm very disappointed in you, Brenda,' he'd said in his sternest voice. 'Fancy digging a hole in the middle of the lawn! I thought you were much more sensible than that.'

'I'm sorry, Dad,' Brenda had replied, staring hard at her feet and trying not to cry. 'It – it won't happen again.'

'You're darn right, it won't happen again!' Dad had snapped.

The next day, straight after lunch, Dad went out in the car on his own. He came back, an hour later, with the car boot full of what looked like giant chocolate swiss rolls with mint cream filling.

Brenda watched from the front door as he unloaded them. They weren't swiss rolls; they were strips of earth with grass on.

'What are they?' Brenda asked Mum.

'Turfs,' replied Mum. 'To fill up the hole.'

Brenda and Sean watched from the living room as Dad covered up the Brownie Pool with new grass.

Every night for the next week, as soon as he got home from work,

Dad tended and watered the new patch of baby lawn. By the weekend, you couldn't tell that there had ever been a Magic Pool in the garden. In fact, the whole incident seemed to have been forgiven and forgotten.

Brenda decided it was now safe to ask her Mum and Dad about her next great idea.

FOUR

'Mum?' said Brenda, as soon as she'd finished helping to dry up the plates from Sunday lunch. 'Can Sylvia come and stay next Saturday?'

'I don't see why not,' said Mum.

'And you know the tent in the garage, Mum? Can we all sleep in that?'

Mum put the last of the plates in the cupboard, and turned round to Brenda.

'Who – you and Sylvia?'

'And Sean, too,' said Brenda. 'It's ever such a big tent – we'd all fit in . . .'

'I'm not sure that's such a good idea,' said Mum, pursing her lips. 'I think you'd better go and ask your father.'

Brenda's dad was sitting in his

favourite armchair in the sitting room.

'Dad? Can Sylvia come and stay the night, next Saturday?'

Dad smiled at Brenda. It was a sleepy, contented, full-of-roast-beef-and-Yorkshire-pudding smile.

'Yes,' he said, 'as long as Mum doesn't mind. But you'll have to tidy up your room first. I won't be able to get the camp bed in if the floor's covered with Lego and bits of dolls' house furniture.'

Brenda hesitated. This was the tricky bit.

'Well, actually, Dad . . . I was thinking we could sleep outside, like a sort of camp. I thought that me and Sylvia – and Sean, too – could all sleep in the tent.'

'Do you mean the old tent in the garage?' asked Dad.

Brenda nodded.

'I'm not sure that's a very good idea—'

'Oh please, Dad, please? It would be brilliant if we could sleep in the tent! You'd be the best dad in the world if you let us! If we could sleep outside, we could pretend we were camping – just like real Br—'

Oooops! Brenda stopped. She'd almost said the forbidden word.

Dad looked at Brenda suspiciously. 'Were you going to say *Brownies*?'

Brenda blushed.

'Hmmmm . . .' said Dad.

Brenda waited, for what seemed like hours, while Dad thought about the idea.

'If I did say yes, you'd have to promise me that there would be no digging—'

'Yes! I promise!' said Brenda excitedly. 'You're the best dad in the world!'

'Hold on a minute. I haven't said yes yet,' Dad pointed out. 'First, I'll have to look at the tent. We haven't used it properly since before Sean was born. It might be full of holes—'

'Will you look at it now – please, Dad, please?'

'No,' said Dad, firmly.

'Oh, but Dad—'

'Listen to me, Brenda,' said Dad sternly. '*If* I'm going to agree to this camp of yours – and it's a big *If* – you're going to have to be very, very good all week. Understand?'

'Yes, Dad.'

'I will look at the tent, but not just now. I'm going to have a little rest, for the next hour or so. I've had to work hard – and garden hard – all week. So, *if* you want your camp, you'll leave me in peace. OK?'

'Yes, Dad.'

Dad settled down in his armchair.

He put the Business Section of the Sunday paper over his face. Brenda tiptoed from the room as quietly as she could.

'. . . But it wouldn't be a very big camp fire,' Brenda tried to explain.

It was Saturday afternoon. Brenda and her dad were bickering in the garden.

'Absolutely not!' Dad exclaimed. 'I wouldn't dream of letting you have a fire on your own, and I'm certainly not going to spend all night sitting out here to make sure you don't set fire to yourselves. And I know that Sylvia's mother would have a *fit* if she thought you were going to have a bonfire.'

'She wouldn't, Dad,' Brenda pleaded desperately. 'She wouldn't mind at all.'

'NO! And that's *final*!' Dad was getting angry. 'And if you keep

arguing like this – I'll call the whole thing off!'

Mum stood up with a weary groan. While Dad and Brenda had been arguing, she had been fixing the guy ropes of the tent.

'Be reasonable, Brenda,' she said, patiently. 'Dad is quite right. You're much too young to have a bonfire – it's much too dangerous. But I've got an idea: why don't you have a pretend bonfire, instead?'

'How can you have a pretend bonfire?' asked Brenda, grumpily.

'You could use your old Night Light – the one that works on batteries – and your torch, too. You'll need a light in the tent, anyway. You could switch them on, outside the tent, and sit round them and do whatever it is you want to do.'

Brenda didn't say anything. She just looked sulky.

'That's the best I can suggest,' said Mum.

'All right,' Brenda agreed, reluctantly.

'What do you say . . . ?' prompted Dad.

'Thanks, Mum.'

Sylvia arrived at five o'clock. She was carrying a small, pale blue suitcase in one hand and a pale pink pretend handbag in the other. She was wearing her second-best frock.

Brenda had changed into her brown corduroy trousers, brown-and-yellow striped T-shirt and old brown bobble hat. Sean was wearing his Spiderman pyjamas and gun-belt. Tigger wasn't wearing anything, except his fur.

'Thank you for asking me to stay, Mrs Robinson,' said Sylvia politely.

'That's all right, Sylvia,' said

Brenda's mum. 'Take your things outside, and then we'll have tea.'

Sylvia looked puzzled. 'Outside?' she asked.

'Yes, dear,' said Mum. 'Outside in the tent.'

Sylvia looked shocked. 'You mean the tent's *outside*?' she asked.

'Yes, Sylvia,' said Mum patiently, 'in the garden. Didn't Brenda tell you that you'd be sleeping in a tent?'

'Yes,' replied Sylvia, in a worried voice. 'But she didn't say anything about it being outside. I thought it would be in Brenda's room – you know, a pretend tent. I didn't know it was going to be a *real* one!'

As soon as tea was finished, and Brenda and Sylvia had changed into their night things, Brenda led her Brownies out to camp.

Even though it was still light, Brenda lit their way with her Mister Man battery-operated night light.

Sylvia followed, holding up the hem of her dainty pink nightie, and stepping very carefully so that she wouldn't get her new fluffy slippers dirty. Last came Sean, lugging a very grumpy Tigger.

Tigger's tail was swishing from side to side, and he was mewing in a very threatening way. He didn't like being carried by anyone. He particularly didn't like being carried by small, clumsy five-year-old boys who left important bits of him – like his back legs and his front legs – dangling perilously in mid-air. But what he really hated was being dragged away from a half-eaten bowl of Whiskas.

Tigger waited until they were half-way down the garden – then he made his move. Getting a good firm grip on Sean's arm, Tigger launched himself out of Sean's grasp and sprinted back up the garden towards his half-finished supper.

'Ow-oww-oooooh!' wailed Sean. 'He scratched me!'

He pulled up the sleeve of his Spiderman pyjamas and pointed to a neat semi-circle of scarlet dots where Tigger's claws had dug into his arm.

'I want Mum!' he bellowed.

'Don't be such a baby!' Brenda said, in her bossiest Sixer voice. 'Brownies don't cry over a silly little scratch.'

'I don't want to be a Brownie!' howled Sean. 'I want my muummm!'

Mum appeared at the kitchen door and hurried up the path.

'I don't want to be a Brownie!' sobbed Sean, as he ran towards her. 'I want to go home!'

With a weary sigh, Mum scooped Sean up and carried him back towards the house.

Dad was standing in the doorway. He said something to Mum as she carried Sean indoors. Brenda couldn't hear exactly what he said, but it sounded very like, 'I told you so!'

'It'll be much more fun with just us,' said Brenda to Sylvia. 'And there'll be more room in the tent.'

FIVE

'What do we do now?' asked Sylvia, as soon as the two girls had crawled into the tent.

'Lots of really exciting things,' replied Brenda. 'Sing songs, tell stories, and' – she rummaged about underneath her sleeping bag and pulled out a paper bag – 'have a midnight feast!'

'It's getting dark,' said Sylvia, in a worried voice. She clutched Silverhooves tightly.

'Time to switch on the torches,' said Brenda.

'I haven't got a torch,' said Sylvia.

'You can use Sean's.' Brenda produced two torches from behind Sylvia's pillow, and handed one to Sylvia.

They switched them on. The tent

was bathed in a cosy, orange glow. Sylvia relaxed a little.

'Let's start with a sing-song,' said Brenda.

'What shall we sing?' asked Sylvia.

' "She'll be coming round the mountain," ' said Brenda.

'I don't know that song,' said Sylvia.

'It's really good,' said Brenda. 'I'll teach you.'

And she began to sing:

*'She'll be coming round the mountain
 when she comes,
She'll be coming round the mountain
 when she comes.
She'll be coming round the mountain,
Coming round the mountain,
Coming round the mountain when
 she comes.'*

'Is that it?' asked Sylvia, disappointed. 'Just *She'll be coming round the mountain when she comes?*'

'No,' said Brenda. 'After you've sung *She'll be coming round the mountain*, you change the words.'

'What to?' asked Sylvia.

'Oh, all sorts of things,' replied Brenda. *'She'll be wearing pink pyjamas . . .* or *She'll be riding on a push-bike—'*

'That's silly!' said Sylvia. 'You don't wear pyjamas to climb mountains. And you can't ride push-bikes up mountains, either.'

'It's meant to be silly,' explained Brenda. 'It's that sort of song.'

'Well, I don't think it's any good,' said Sylvia, haughtily.

'Have you got any better ideas?' asked Brenda.

Sylvia hadn't. So they sang *She'll be coming round the mountain* – or rather, Brenda sang and Sylvia muttered some of the words. The sing-song fizzled out.

Brenda opened the paper bag.

'Time for the midnight feast!' she announced.

Brenda shook the contents of the bag on to her sleeping-bag. There were six coloured balls of bubble gum in a plastic tube, four twopenny chews, four pink candy shrimps and two green jelly turtles.

Sylvia wrinkled her nose in disgust. 'My mum doesn't let me eat cheap sweets,' she said snootily. 'She says that they're not hygienic unless they're properly wrapped.'

'They're not cheap!' Brenda protested. 'They cost me thirty pence – all my pocket money!'

Sylvia looked at the sweets and sniffed.

'Don't you even want some bubble gum?' asked Brenda. 'That's wrapped.'

'My mum *never* lets me eat bubble gum!' replied Sylvia, in a shocked voice. 'She says that if you swallow bubble gum you'll choke, and it all gets knotted up inside you.'

'I don't believe you!'

'It's true!' insisted Sylvia. 'My mum says that there are stories in the paper every day about children who swallow bubble gum and end up in hospital. And they have to eat through a tube in their noses – for the rest of their lives!'

Brenda still didn't quite believe her, but she decided to leave the bubble gum till later. She popped two pink shrimps into her mouth. They tasted delicious! Finally, Sylvia nibbled a twopenny chew while Brenda polished off the two remaining shrimps, three chews and two jelly turtles.

'What shall we do now?' asked Sylvia.

'Tell stories,' said Brenda. 'You first.'

'But I don't know any stories,' said Sylvia.

'Well, make one up,' said Brenda.

'All right . . .' said Sylvia, uncertainly. There was a long pause as Sylvia thought. 'Erm . . . once upon a time there was a king and queen. And they lived in a great big castle. They wanted a baby to be their princess, but they didn't have one for years and years and years. And when they did, a bad fairy came along and said: "When this child is ten years old, she will prick her finger on a spinning wheel—" '

'You're not making this up,' said Brenda.

'I am, too!' insisted Sylvia.

'Are not!' said Brenda. 'It's *The Sleeping Beauty*.'

'Isn't . . .' said Sylvia, uncertainly.

'Is, too!' said Brenda. 'Anyway, that's not the right kind of story. When you're on a camp, you have to tell scary stories – stories about ghosts, and werewolves, and

vampires, and Frankenstein monsters!'

'I don't know any,' said Sylvia in a small voice.

'Well, I do,' said Brenda proudly. 'But before I start you have to turn your torch off.'

'Do I have to?' asked Sylvia nervously.

'Yes,' said Brenda.

Sylvia switched her torch off. Brenda held her torch under her chin. It threw an eerie light on to Brenda's face, so that her eyes and the tip of her nose glowed spookily. The rest of her face – and the tent around them – was half hidden in menacing shadows. In a slow, deep voice, Brenda began her story:

'Once upon a time there was a dark, dark, wood' – and as she said the words 'dark, dark wood' she made her voice go all trembly, like an owl's hoot – 'and in the middle of the dark, dark wood was a dark, dark bridge. And over the dark, dark bridge was a dark, dark path. And the dark, dark path led to a dark, dark clearing in the dark, dark wood. And in the middle of the dark, dark clearing was a dark, dark cottage.' Sylvia sat mesmerized by the chanting and the ghostly glow on Brenda's face. 'And in the front of the dark, dark cottage was a dark, dark door,' continued Brenda. 'And through the dark, dark door was a dark, dark stairway. At the top of the dark, dark stairs was a dark, dark passage. At the end of the dark, dark passage was a dark, dark room. In the dark, dark room was a dark, dark corner. And in the dark, dark corner was a dark, dark coffin. And in the dark, dark coffin was a dark, dark skeleton which said—'

And, without warning, Brenda snapped off the torch, grabbed

Sylvia by the wrist and screeched, 'GOTCHER!'

'Aiieeeeee!' screamed Sylvia, frightened out of her wits. 'Eeeeeaiiiii!'

Sylvia tried desperately to scramble out of the tent, but Brenda was between her and the flap.

'Aaaaaargh!' shrieked Brenda. 'Let go – that's my hair!'

'Eeeeeeiyargh!' yelled Sylvia. 'Let me go! Let me out! *Let me out!*'

'Owwwwwww!' yelled Brenda. 'You're on my fingers! Aaaaaaargh! Get off!'

'*Help!*' screamed Sylvia.

'AAAAAIIIEEEEEE!' screamed both girls together.

There was the sound of running feet, and the tent-flap was suddenly wrenched open. The two howling girls were hauled out of the tent by Brenda's dad. Mum was standing behind him.

'What *on earth* is going on?' asked Dad.

'She told me a horrible story and turned out all the lights and grabbed me!' howled Sylvia.

'She pulled my hair and stamped on my fingers!' sobbed Brenda.

'Stop this noise AT ONCE!' yelled Dad, louder than both of them.

'I think we've had quite enough camping for one night,' said Mum calmly. 'Come indoors, the pair of you. You can both sleep in Brenda's room, instead.'

Mum led the way up the path, by the light of the Mister Man Night Light. Sylvia followed, holding Mum's hand. Brenda – sucking her poor bruised fingers – followed behind with Dad.

And, although it was dark, Brenda was sure that when Sylvia looked back she was smiling a small triumphant smile.

SIX

'Salt – mustard – vinegar – pepper!' chanted Brenda and Sylvia together. 'Salt – mustard – vinegar – pepper!'

Their two skipping ropes slap-slapped in time on the pavement.

'Salt – mustard – vinegar – '

But before she could get to 'pepper' again, Brenda's rope snagged against her right heel and she stumbled and stopped.

Sylvia kept on skipping: 'Salt – mustard – vinegar – pepper . . .'

Brenda flopped down on the low wall outside Sylvia's house. She needed a rest. It was a hot day for skipping – besides, they'd been skipping for almost an hour and Brenda was getting bored.

Sylvia wasn't. Sylvia *never* got bored with skipping.

'Salt – mustard – vinegar – pepper!' she chanted. 'Salt – mustard – vinegar – *beat you*!' Sylvia beamed triumphantly at Brenda.

It was Saturday morning, two weeks after the camping fiasco. Dad had taken Sean into town to buy him a new pair of shoes. They would probably be gone all day. Buying shoes for Sean involved a lot of screaming, yelling and arguing. Sean was the person who did most of the screaming, yelling and arguing – but not all of it. Brenda was very glad she didn't have to go, too – despite all the skipping.

The skipping had been Mum's idea.

'I *must* get the bedrooms spring cleaned,' she'd said. 'Every time I start, something always happens to interrupt me.'

'Can I help?' asked Brenda eagerly.

'Yes,' said Mum. 'You can be

really helpful by going out to play and letting me get on with it in peace. Look' – she pointed out of the window – 'Sylvia's outside skipping. Why don't you take your skipping rope and go and join her. You could have a skipping competition! It's a lovely sunny day. You don't want to be inside, do you?'

And before Brenda could argue, she found she had a skipping rope in her hand and was being gently shooed outside on to the pavement.

'Salt – mustard – vinegar – pepper! Salt – mustard – vinegar . . .'

Brenda watched as Sylvia's rope looped gracefully up and down. With her steady, clockwork pace Sylvia could keep going for hours and hours and hours . . .

Then Brenda noticed two girls standing by the post box at the corner of the road. They were both

dressed in neat, blue uniforms: Girl Guides. One girl was holding a flat brown box; the other girl was rattling a tin. They must have arrived during the Great Skipping Marathon.

Brenda rolled up her skipping rope, put it carefully on the wall, and hurried up the road to investigate.

'Hallo,' said the Guide with the tin. She rattled it under Brenda's nose. 'Do you want to buy a flag?'

'Erm . . . I don't know,' replied Brenda. She looked into the cardboard tray which the other Guide held out to her. But there weren't any flags on the tray, only little circular pieces of sticky paper with a picture of a dog and some writing on each.

Brenda looked down on the ground, then tried to peer behind the Guides, looking for another box with flags in. There wasn't one.

'Where are they?' asked Brenda.

'Where are what?' asked the Guide with the tin.

'The flags,' replied Brenda.

The Guide with the box laughed and pointed to the little stickers. 'These are the flags,' she said. 'I don't know why they're called flags, but they are.'

'How much are they?' asked Brenda, a little disappointed. She'd been expecting brightly coloured Union Jacks, the sort you put on the top of sandcastles. Or even better, a real cloth Scottish flag with a big red lion on.

'Whatever you can afford,' said the Guide with the tin. 'Most people give us ten pence.'

Brenda looked shocked. Ten pence for a small round picture of a dog! It seemed very expensive.

'We're collecting money for the Greenwood Animal Shelter,'

explained the Guide with the box. 'And we give one of these stickers to anyone who gives us money.'

Greenwood Animal Shelter? Brenda was confused. An animal shelter? What was that? She knew what a bus shelter was. Could an animal shelter be the same sort of thing, but specially for animals who were travelling on their own, and made of green wood instead of concrete and glass? It didn't seem very likely.

'Have you heard of the Animal Shelter?' asked the Guide with the box.

Brenda shook her head.

'Well, an animal shelter is like a home for animals that are hurt or whose owners don't want them any more,' explained the Guide.

The other Guide rattled her tin. 'Do you want to help?' she asked. 'All the money goes to buy food and things for the animals.'

'Oh, yes!' said Brenda, enthusiastically. But then her face fell. 'But I haven't any money . . .'

The Guide with the box thought for a moment.

'That doesn't matter. Maybe you've got some jumble,' she suggested. 'You know – old clothes, old books, toys and games you don't want any more. You see, we're collecting money like this. But the Brownies are holding a jumble sale this afternoon. If you've got any jumble, you can take it along to the church hall. The Brownies will sell it, and all the money will go to the Animal Shelter.'

She turned to her friend.

'I think we should try the next road,' she said. 'We haven't collected anything here.'

Then she turned back to Brenda. 'Bye-bye,' she said. 'And don't forget about the jumble sale.'

'No,' said Brenda. 'I won't!'

Brenda was almost bursting with excitement: a real Brownie jumble sale – and they needed *her* help! This was a chance for Brenda to show that she could be as kind and helpful to the poor animals who were ill or had no homes as the real Brownies. A plan quickly formed in Brenda's mind: she and Sylvia would find lots and lots of jumble. They would find more jumble than anyone else, and the Brownies would be so grateful and *so* impressed.

As she walked back to where Sylvia was skipping, Brenda imagined the scene at the church hall when she and Sylvia staggered in with bags and bags and boxes and boxes of toys, books and clothes: Brown Owl wiping away tears of gratitude; all the Brownies cheering and clapping.

'Without you, Brenda, our jumble sale would have been useless,'

Brown Owl was saying. 'But thanks to all your wonderful things – it's going to be the best jumble sale we've ever had!'

And then Brown Owl would beg – yes, beg – Brenda to join the Brownie Pack immediately.

'I can see that you'll make such a wonderful Brownie, that I want you to be a Sixer straight away!'

And all the Brownies cheered and sang 'For She's a Jolly Good Fellow!'

Brenda walked slowly down the road towards Sylvia, lost in her daydream.

Sylvia was still skipping: 'Salt – mustard – vinegar . . .' so Brenda sat on the wall. By the time Sylvia finally got fed up with skipping and came and sat down on the wall, the Brownie Pack was carrying Brenda round the church hall – shoulder high – cheering and cheering, and throwing their bobble hats in the air!

SEVEN

Brenda's mum was still in the bedroom when the two girls rushed excitedly into the house.

'Mum, Mum!' yelled Brenda. 'The Brownies are having a—'

'Please, Brenda,' said Mum, 'I haven't got time to talk about Brownies now – can't you see I'm busy?'

'But, Mum—'

'I said no, Brenda.' Mum looked hot and frazzled. The spring cleaning didn't seem to have gone very well: the room looked more untidy than when she'd started. There were piles of clothes all over the floor.

'It's hopeless!' complained Mum. 'I don't know why we keep all these clothes. Just look at all these suits . . .' She pointed to a huge pile on the floor. 'I don't know why your father needs so many,' she said to Brenda. 'He hardly ever wears them. I've a good mind to send them to a jumble sale!'

'But, Mum, that's what I've been trying—'

But Mum wasn't listening. She'd caught sight of the clock beside her bed. 'Good heavens! Is that the time? You must be starving – it's nearly one—'

'But, Mum, can me and Sylvia—'

'All right,' said Mum with a sigh. 'Sylvia can stay to lunch. But it'll only be something quick – spaghetti rings on toast, or something.'

'Thank you very much, Mrs Robinson,' said Sylvia.

'But, *Mum*,' Brenda tried again. 'The Brownies are—'

'If you want to be good and helpful, like the Brownies,' Mum interrupted, 'you can start by putting some of these clothes back in the wardrobe while I get lunch. Will you do that?'

And without waiting for a reply, Mum rushed downstairs to the kitchen.

Brenda and Sylvia began to put the trousers and heavy jackets on to hangers. But when they opened the wardrobe door, the wardrobe seemed to be crammed full with Brenda's mum's trousers and jackets and skirts and dresses.

'Doesn't your mum ever throw anything away?' asked Sylvia, surprised. 'My mum throws *all* her old clothes away, every year, and buys all new ones!'

'I don't believe you,' said Brenda.

'Well . . . almost all her clothes,' Sylvia corrected herself. 'But my dad doesn't. That's why she shouts at him so much,' she added proudly.

After a lot of effort, they managed to squeeze two thin jackets and a pair of cord jeans into the crowded wardrobe. The pile of clothes on the floor looked as large as when they'd started. They stared at the pile.

'Do you think your mum meant it – about sending your dad's clothes to a jumble sale?' asked Sylvia.

'I don't know.' Brenda shrugged. 'She says that every time she spring cleans . . . but she never does anything. Let's go and ask!' she said excitedly.

The two girls went downstairs to the kitchen.

'Mum?' said Brenda.

Mum had just opened a tin of spaghetti rings. She hadn't heard Brenda and Sylvia come in. She jumped in surprise, and the tin skidded off the worktop and landed face down on the floor.

'Oh, blast! Look what you made

me do,' scolded Mum. She ran across the kitchen and grabbed a cloth from the sink. Just as she was bending down to clear up the mess, Brenda noticed smoke coming from under the grill.

'Mum – something's burning!'

'Oh, no! The toast!'

Mum dropped the cloth and leapt towards the oven. Thick black smoke was curling up from under the grill.

The doorbell rang.

'See who that is at the door,' said Mum to Brenda and Sylvia. 'And tell them to call back later . . .'

The two girls rushed to the front door. Brenda opened it. Standing on the step were two Brownies. Outside the front gate was an older girl, of about thirteen or fourteen. She was holding the handle of a large wooden handcart. On the cart was an untidy pile of cardboard boxes and bulging plastic bin liners.

'Hallo,' said one of the Brownies. 'We're collecting for the jumble sale in the church hall this afternoon. It's to raise money for the Greenwood Animal Shelter. Have you got anything we can have?'

Brenda and Sylvia looked at each other.

'I'll just ask my mum,' said Brenda.

The two girls rushed excitedly back to the kitchen.

'Mum! Mum! It's the Brownies! They're collecting for the Animal Shelter, and—'

Brenda's mum was on her hands and knees trying to mop up a large pool of sticky tomato sauce.

'Please, Brenda,' said Mum, 'can't you see I can't do anything at the moment?'

'But, Mum, they're collecting for

the poor animals who haven't got any homes and are ill.'

Brenda's mum heaved a weary sigh. 'I think there's some small change in my coat, hanging up in the hall. Give them something.'

'But, Mum,' began Brenda. 'They want—'

'I know what they want!' snapped Mum. 'Just give them something – and please don't bother me again. Let me get on with cleaning up this mess – or we'll never get any lunch!'

Brenda and Sylvia rushed back to the front door.

'Yes!' said Brenda, excitedly. 'We've got *lots* of things for your jumble sale!'

'What would you like for sweet?' asked Brenda's mum, when they'd finished their beans on toast. 'Yoghurt, or . . .' she peered into the fridge, '. . . yoghurt.'

As Brenda and Sylvia peeled the tops off their yoghurts, Mum asked, 'Those Brownies – how much did you give them?'

'Everything,' replied Brenda.

'Yes – but how much was that?' asked Mum.

'Everything,' repeated Brenda.

'Yes – but how much? How much money was in my coat?'

'Oh, we didn't give them your coat, Mrs Robinson,' said Sylvia.

Brenda's mum laughed. 'No, of course you didn't, dear. But you did give them some money, didn't you?'

'Oh, no,' replied Brenda. 'They weren't collecting money.'

'But I thought you said—'

'No, Mum,' explained Brenda. 'They were collecting for the jumble sale this afternoon in the church hall.'

'But you said you gave them . . .' The smile slowly drained from

Brenda's mum's face like bathwater running away.

'Everything,' repeated Brenda. 'All Dad's clothes – like you said.'

'You did WHAT?' shrieked Brenda's mum, and without waiting for a reply she tore out of the kitchen and pounded up the stairs.

'I don't think . . .' began Sylvia.

'*Brenda!* Come up here!' yelled Mum from upstairs.

'. . . your Mum's very pleased,' said Sylvia.

They got to the church hall just before the sale was about to start. The doors were shut, but there was already a long queue outside. Brenda's mum led Brenda and Sylvia past the long line of people to the head of the queue. Two old ladies were at the very front.

'Excuse me,' said Brenda's mother

politely. 'Can we get through, please?'

But the two old ladies were deep in conversation, and didn't seem to hear her.

'. . . last week's was a good one,' one old lady was saying to the other. 'Red Cross – you always get good jumble at the Red Cross. I got meself three pairs of thermal bloomers – fleecy lined, too. They should last me all next winter!'

'Yes, but we were too late for the vests,' grumbled the other old lady. 'There wasn't a single string vest left by the time we arrived. That's what I'm looking for today – a couple of nice string vests for him indoors.'

'I'm sorry, but can we get past?' asked Brenda's mum again. 'I've got to get in before the sale starts.'

The two old ladies glared at her.

'What's your game, eh?' asked the first old lady, suspiciously. 'Go to

the back. Can't you see there's a queue?'

'I do apologize,' said Brenda's mother squeezing past them. 'But there's been a terrible mistake . . .'

'Blooming cheek!' declared the first old lady.

'I know your sort!' the second old lady yelled after them. 'Pinching all the vests before anyone else gets a chance!'

Brenda's mum steered Brenda and Sylvia past the protesting old ladies, through the door, and into the church hall.

Brown Owl was sitting at a small table by the door. She stood up as Mum, Brenda and Sylvia came in.

'I'm sorry,' she said, 'but you'll have to wait outside with all the others. We're not starting the sale for another quarter of an hour.'

'We're not here to buy anything . . .' explained Brenda's

mum, and she quickly told Brown
Owl about the suits, and how they'd
been sent by mistake.

Brown Owl led them over to the
Second-Hand Men's Clothes stall.
'Which one's were they?' she asked.

'The black one with the stripes,'
said Brenda's mum, pointing. 'The
blue one, that brown one and the
grey one with the checks. And the
green tweed sports jacket, the dark
blue trousers . . . Oh, yes, and the
two pairs of grey trousers hanging on
the end.'

Brown Owl looked shocked. 'Is
that everything?' she asked.

'I think so . . .' said Mum. 'No,
there was a dinner jacket and a pair
of black trousers with a shiny stripe
down each leg.'

Brown Owl looked behind the
stall.

'Yes, here it is,' she said. 'Oh dear,
it seems to have got a bit muddy.'

'Sorry, Brown Owl,' said one of the Brownies behind the stall. 'It fell off the handcart, and . . . erm, the wheels went over it.'

Brown Owl helped them to pack up all the suits into two big plastic sacks. Brenda's mum took one sack, Brenda and Sylvia carried the other.

As they reached the door, the church clock struck the half hour, and the Brownie nearest the door opened it to let in the waiting bargain hunters.

The two old ladies were first in.

'It's her!' said the first old lady to her friend. 'The one who pushed past us. Blooming sauce!'

'Did you see those bags she was carrying?' asked the other old lady. 'Full of vests – you mark my words!'

EIGHT

When Dad heard about the suits he was very cross. He got even more cross when he found the price stickers.

'Look at this!' he complained to Mum, when Brenda was in bed. 'One pound fifty! My best suit! It cost two hundred and fifty pounds, and they were going to sell it for *one pound fifty pence*!'

'Ssssh, dear,' said Brenda's mum. 'Don't get so upset . . .'

Brenda lay in bed, and listened to Dad fuming. A big tear rolled down her cheek. She'd tried *so* hard to help everybody: the poor animals who were sick and had no homes; and Mum and Dad, too, by getting rid of Dad's old clothes. Mum *had* said she wanted Dad's suits sent to a jumble sale. But everything had gone wrong again, and now Dad was getting cross with Mum!

'It's all my fault,' thought Brenda. 'But what can I do to make things better?'

'And another thing,' she heard Dad exclaim, from downstairs, 'I need that evening suit for next Friday. The dry cleaners will never get it cleaned in time, it's all covered in mud . . .'

'I wonder if there's anything in *The Brownie Guide Handbook* about what to do when things go wrong,' thought Brenda. She got out of bed, and took it off her bookshelf. She flicked through the pages until she came to a chapter with the heading: 'How Are Your Ventures Going?'

'Terrible!' muttered Brenda, and she began to read it. But there didn't seem to be anything on the first two pages about disasters or catastrophes, just suggestions about running-and-jumping competitions, and making dolls' clothes. She turned over the page – and there was her answer! At the top of the page was a picture of two Brownie arms up to their elbows in a bowl of soapy water. Above the picture, Brenda read the words: 'Have You Some Good Washerwomen in the Pack?'

'That's *it*!' thought Brenda. 'I'll clean Dad's suit myself. I'll get up extra early tomorrow, and I'll wash all the mud off. Then I'll make Mum and Dad breakfast in bed. That's what a real Brownie would do – and that's what I'll do!'

She settled down to go to sleep. 'Wake up early . . . wake up early . . . wake up early,' she murmured to herself. 'Wake up early . . . wake up early . . . yawn! . . . wake up . . .'

★ ★ ★

Brenda did wake up early. As she got out of bed, she saw that the clock on her wall said six o'clock. Brenda put on her dressing-gown and slippers, and tiptoed down the stairs, along the hall and into the kitchen.

The plastic bag with the dirty evening suit in it was slumped on the floor in a corner of the kitchen, where Mum had put it the night before.

Brenda took the suit out and spread it on the floor. It was filthy! It was covered in mud, and there were two oily black lines across the front of the jacket where it had been run over by the cartwheels.

Brenda shook her head. Her plan had been to wash the dirt off with a sponge, but the jacket was much too grubby for that.

'It'll have to go in the washing machine,' thought Brenda.

She opened the door of the

95

washing machine and crammed the suit in. She carefully sprinkled half a packet of washing powder over the dirty suit, then shut the door. All that remained was to switch on . . . but that was the next big problem: there was no switch that said 'On'. There was a red button, a green button, and a little red light. There was a large dial with lots of squiggles and symbols all around it, and there was a large metal handle that opened and closed the door. But no matter how hard Brenda looked, she couldn't find anything that said 'On' or 'Start' or 'Go'.

'This is no good,' muttered Brenda. 'What use is a washing machine that won't wash. I'll try the green button – green means "Go" on traffic lights.'

She pushed the green button. Nothing happened.

She pushed the red button.
Nothing happened.

Then, just as she was about to give up, Brenda saw the dishwasher. On the front of the dishwasher was a large button which said 'Wash'.

'If it washes dishes, it must be able to wash clothes too,' thought Brenda.

She opened the washing machine, pulled the dirty suit out, and dragged it across the kitchen floor to the dishwasher. Then she opened the front of the dishwasher, and crammed the suit inside. She sprinkled in the rest of the packet of washing powder, closed the front of the dishwasher, and pressed the 'Wash' button.

Instantly, there came the familiar sound of water filling the machine, followed by a purr which meant that the wash cycle had begun.

'Success at last!' thought Brenda. 'Now for the surprise breakfast . . .'

★ ★ ★

'John – John! Wake up.' Mum poked Dad in the ribs.

'Waarghf! Wassermatter? What time is it?'

'Ssssh!' said Mum. 'Listen – can you hear it?'

'Hear what?' asked Dad.

'A noise,' replied Mum.

'What noise?'

'*That* noise,' said Mum. 'It's coming from downstairs.'

'It's just the dishwasher,' said Dad. 'It's nothing to worry about – go back to sleep.'

'But it's *half-past six in the morning*,' Mum said. 'Why's the dishwasher going at this time?'

'I don't know,' said Dad grumpily. 'Maybe you switched it on last night and forgot about it?'

'No,' said Mum, shaking her head. 'I'm certain I didn't. I think we should go and see what's happening.

It may have broken down; it might be flooding the kitchen!'

Dad rubbed his eyes. 'OK,' he agreed reluctantly, 'let's go and see what's happening.'

In the kitchen, Brenda had almost finished getting the surprise breakfast ready for Mum and Dad. On the tray were two glasses of orange juice, and some crackers spread with marmalade. She was just pouring cereal into two bowls when Mum and Dad appeared in the doorway.

'Oh, dear,' said Brenda, 'you've spoilt the surprise. I was going to bring you breakfast in bed, to . . . erm, say sorry about the jumble sale and everything.'

'How sweet of you,' said Mum, smiling. 'And you're doing the washing-up, too – how thoughtful!'

'Wait a minute . . .' said Dad. 'I've just remembered. *I* did the

washing-up last night, before we came to bed. So what . . . ?'

'That was the other part of the surprise,' Brenda explained. 'I'm cleaning your suit, so you can wear it next Friday.'

'WHAT!' yelled Dad. 'My evening suit – in the . . . in the . . . *dishwasher*!'

Dad ran across the kitchen, switched off the dishwasher, and yanked open the door. A tidal wave of soapy water gushed out of the machine, soaking Dad's pyjamas and spreading quickly across the kitchen floor.

'My best suit!' wailed Dad, as he hauled the sodden black mess out of the machine. 'It's . . . *ruined*!'

'Oh!' cried Brenda. 'I'm so sorry . . . I was only trying to help . . . I was only trying to do what a real Brownie—'

'I think it would be a good idea,

Brenda, if you didn't say another word,' said Mum, in a very slow, clear, quiet voice. 'If I were you,' she continued, 'I would go up to my bedroom and stay there!'

Brenda lay on her bed, staring at the ceiling. She'd been doing that for hours: staring at the ceiling . . . and crying. There was a large damp patch on her pillow from her tears.

'It's not fair,' she said to herself. 'Everything I do always turns out wrong. I was only trying to help; I was only trying to be a good Brownie – like it said in the book. And now everything's . . . everything's . . . *awful*!'

She turned her face to the pillow and sobbed.

A minute or two later, the bedroom door opened and Mum came in. She walked over to the bed and put her arms round Brenda.

'Come on, love, cheer up,' Mum murmured in a soothing voice. 'Dad and I know you were trying to do your best . . . it's just that, well, you shouldn't have tried to do all those things on your own – without help. Why do you think Brownies have Brown Owls and people like that? I'll tell you: it's to stop things going wrong; to stop all the Brownies getting themselves into trouble. Here—'

Mum gave her a hanky. Brenda wiped her eyes and blew her nose loudly.

'I think it will be safest for everybody if you started Brownies next Monday,' continued Mum, 'before something even worse happens.'

Brenda sat up, with a look of astonishment on her face.

'Brown Owl agrees with me,'

Mum added. 'I've just spoken to her on the phone.'

'But I thought you said . . . well, that she *couldn't* take any more Brownies.' Brenda was bewildered.

'She couldn't, until she got another helper. And now she has,' said Mum, with a smile. 'Me! We made a deal: if I become an Owl, you can become a Brownie!'

Brenda sat up and gave her mum a great big hug.

'Oh, Mum! Thank you, thank you, thank you! It's going to be brilliant fun – you'll see!'

'I hope so,' said Mum, 'I hope so . . .'

All Pan books are available at your local bookshop or newsagent, or can be ordered direct from the publisher. Indicate the number of copies required and fill in the form below.

Send to: **CS Department, Pan Books Ltd., P.O. Box 40, Basingstoke, Hants. RG21 2YT.**

or phone: 0256 469551 (Ansaphone), quoting title, author and Credit Card number.

Please enclose a remittance* to the value of the cover price plus: 60p for the first book plus 30p per copy for each additional book ordered to a maximum charge of £2.40 to cover postage and packing.

*Payment may be made in sterling by UK personal cheque, postal order, sterling draft or international money order, made payable to Pan Books Ltd.

Alternatively by Barclaycard/Access:

Card No. | | | | | | | | | | | | | | | | |

Signature:

Applicable only in the UK and Republic of Ireland.

While every effort is made to keep prices low, it is sometimes necessary to increase prices at short notice. Pan Books reserve the right to show on covers and charge new retail prices which may differ from those advertised in the text or elsewhere.

NAME AND ADDRESS IN BLOCK LETTERS PLEASE:

....

Name— Mhairi

Address—